Little Red Riding Hood

retold by Candice Ransom   illustrated by Tammie Lyon

Copyright © 2002 Carson-Dellosa Publishing, LLC. Published by Brighter Child®, an imprint of Carson-Dellosa Publishing, LLC.
Send all inquiries to: Carson-Dellosa Publishing, LLC, P.O. Box 35665, Greensboro, NC 27425.

Printed in the USA.   ISBN 978-1-57768-198-4   17-326167784

**A** long time ago, there lived a sweet little girl who was thoughtful and kind and loved to visit her grandmother.

Her grandmother enjoyed the visits so much that she gave the little girl a special present.

She sewed the girl a wool cape
with a hood. It was the girl's favorite
color, a wonderful cherry red.

The girl liked her cape so much that she wore it everywhere.
First, she wore it to the village store.

Then, she wore it to visit her cousins on the other side of the village.

She even wore her cape to bed! Soon everyone called her Little Red Riding Hood.

One day Little Red Riding Hood's mother said, "Your grandmother isn't feeling well."

"I'll go visit her," said Little Red Riding Hood. "And I'll take a picnic."

"What a good idea," said Little Red Riding Hood's mother. "And be sure to stay on the path through the woods."

Little Red Riding Hood promised that she would, and she packed a basket with her grandmother's favorite foods and set off.

Little Red Riding Hood skipped down the long, winding path as she always did on her visits. And she was very careful to always stay on the path.

After a while, she met a wolf.

"Hello," said the wolf.

Little Red Riding Hood knew she shouldn't talk to the wolf, but he seemed friendly.

"Hello," she said.

"Where are you going this fine day, little girl?" asked the wolf.

"I'm going to visit my grandmother," said Little Red Riding Hood. "She isn't feeling well, so I'm bringing her this picnic with her favorite foods."

"And where does your grandmother live?" asked the wolf.

"At the end of this path."

A sly grin came over the wolf's face.

He knew that if he ran up the hill, he'd get to the grandmother's house before Little Red Riding Hood. *I'll gobble up the old lady and the little girl*, he thought, smacking his lips. *And I'll gobble up that tasty picnic, too!*

"Look at all the flowers growing in the woods," said the crafty wolf. "Why don't you pick some for your grandmother? Pretty flowers will make her feel even better."

"Good idea!" said Little Red Riding Hood.

The prettiest flowers were far from the path. But Little Red Riding Hood thought that it would be all right to leave the path just this once.

When she turned to pick some flowers, the wolf ran straight to the grandmother's house.

The door was unlocked, so the wolf opened it quietly and
crept inside.

He tiptoed into the grandmother's bedroom and found her asleep
in bed. Suddenly she woke up. When she saw the wolf, she screamed!

"Help! Help!" cried Little Red Riding Hood's grandmother.

The wolf grabbed her, pushed her into the closet, and locked the door.

"Be quiet," he said, "or I'll gobble you up now instead of later!"

The wolf quickly put on a nightgown and a cap.
He hopped into bed and pulled the covers up to his
hairy chin.

At that moment, Little Red Riding Hood knocked on the front door.
"Grandmother!" she called.
"Come in, my dear," said the wolf in a high voice.

Little Red Riding Hood went into the bedroom. She stared at her grandmother lying in bed. Her grandmother looked very strange, and Little Red Riding Hood was afraid.

"Grandmother, what big ears you have!" said Little Red Riding Hood.

"The better to hear you with, my dear," said the wolf.

"Grandmother, what big eyes you have!" said Little Red Riding Hood.

"The better to see you with, my dear," said the wolf.

"Grandmother, what big hands you have!" said Little Red Riding Hood.

"The better to hug you with, my dear."

"Grandmother, what big TEETH you have!" said Little Red Riding Hood.

"The better to eat you with!" cried the wolf.

Little Red Riding Hood screamed. This was not her Grandmother. It was the wolf.

Suddenly, the wolf sprang out of bed. He tried to grab Little Red Riding Hood, but she leaped away, light as a leaf in her cherry red cape. The wolf grabbed the air instead!

With a yelp, the wolf tumbled out the window and rolled head over heels down the hill. He was never seen again.

Little Red Riding Hood's grandmother pounded on the closet door. Little Red Riding Hood let her out, and they hugged as tightly as they could.

"Thank goodness that's over with," said her grandmother. "What happened?"

"Mother said you were sick," said Little Red Riding Hood, "so I brought you a picnic lunch. But I left the path to pick flowers."

"Well, I think you've learned your lesson," said her grandmother. "I'm just glad we're both safe."

Then Little Red Riding Hood and her grandmother sat down and enjoyed their visit together. It was the best one they'd ever had.